U0049459

恭 喜 畢 業

離 開 學 校 後 ， 最 重 要 的 事

Congratulations, by the way
Some Thoughts on Kindness

喬治 · 桑德斯
George Saunders

徐之野 譯

獻給我記憶中慈愛的祖父母與外祖父母

約翰・克拉克與珍・克拉克

喬治・桑德斯與瑪麗・桑德斯

關於作者

喬治·桑德斯

(1958-)

美國當代傑出短篇小說家、《紐約時報》暢銷作家。出版過短篇小說集 *CivilWarLand in Bad Decline* (1996)、*Pastoralia* (2000) 以 及 *In Persuasion Nation* (2006)。並以小說《十二月十日》*Tenth of December* 榮獲第一屆佛立歐文學獎 (Folio)，該書也是《紐約時報》暢銷書。

桑德斯並被《TIME》時代雜誌評選為 2013 年年度百大影響人物。他在雪城大學教授文學創作，固定替《GQ 雜誌》、《哈潑雜誌》、《紐約客》寫稿。

早年，桑德斯以暢銷的童書 *The Very Persistent Gappers of Frip* (2000) 獲得圖書獎項肯定。後來投入短篇小說創作，並在國際文壇引起注目，作品陸續被收錄在歐亨利小說獎作品集、最佳美國短篇小說集，並獲得麥克亞瑟天才獎，四度榮獲美國國家雜誌獎，成為屢獲殊榮的小說家。

桑德斯有許多作品延續了喬治·歐威爾式的荒謬諷刺風格，因為曾經在大公司工作的親身體驗，他的作品對資本主義擁護求利求榮，缺乏人與人的情感多所批判，但又能兼具詼諧幽默。他的小說也經常被人拿來跟美國重要作家柯特·馮內果 (Kurt Vonnegut) 相比，相較於馮內果的憤世嫉俗，桑德斯在作品中持續對人保持希望。他曾透過筆下一位失意沮喪的人物說：繼續活下去、與親人保持聯繫，因為「生活中依然可能有很多──很多點點滴滴的善良。」

名人推薦

這篇對就要進入社會的大學畢業生的講演，告訴正準備往前衝的年輕人，最值得追求的美滿人生是「與人為善」，做一個真正的善良人，而不是「功成名就」。我讀了也感到震撼。這是一篇最值得年輕人一讀的講演稿。──林良

小學六年級時，那位渾身髒兮兮、全身流膿流血、被老師責罵、被同學排擠、整天哭哭啼啼的同學，一直在心中從未走遠。一直到現在，我還忍不住想著：他現在過得好嗎？

感謝作者提醒了我們：人生最本質的快樂，來自於對他人及時表達善意。這句經歲月焠鍊的智慧話語，正是讓我們在夜深人靜時仍能身心安穩的最大畢業賀禮。──蘇明進

當知識不再是力量的時代來臨，具備整合創新、關懷利他和挫折容忍的能力，才是未來社會在等待的人才。──徐建國（麗山高中校長）

學校畢業，正是生涯旅程的開始，為行囊中添加智慧。
──賀陳弘（清大校長）

不要怕輸在起跑點，因為你永遠都有機會超越。
──李慶宗（成功中學校長）

誠樸以立，止於至善，作一個體貼、感恩、慈悲的世界公民。
──周景揚（中央大學校長）

媒體推薦

給未來畢業生最好的人生指引之禮。——*Amazon*

如詩篇一樣輕盈,但卻深厚無以倫比。——*The New York Times*

許多人大學畢業時代也許只想聽到接著該怎麼賺錢,但如果要在鍊金術之外聽到一點真心坦率的人生智言,那沒有比這本書作得更棒的了!——*Entertainment Weekly*

桑德斯對人們建議去無私地愛和他所指出人與人間的交互關聯,實在是最純靜最簡單,但也最艱鉅的人生道理。——*Kirkus Reviews*

暖心又溫柔的一本書。——*Publishers Weekly*

緣起

每當畢業季開始，美國各大學府就會邀請社會重要人士蒞臨，為將要
踏上夢想之路的年輕人演講。這些來自各行各業的講者常常會提到人
生中哪些經歷形塑了他們的道路，哪些想法支持他們至今。賈伯斯在
史丹佛大學說的名言「Stay hungry. Stay foolish.」、貝佐斯在普林斯頓
大學以一段年幼往事，教誨世人同理心對很多人來說比聰明更困難。
而這本書則是美國小說家喬治·桑德斯在母校雪城大學（Syracuse
University）的演講內容。

演講中，桑德斯聊起他人生中最後悔的什麼。即使犯過各種錯、闖過
年輕人會闖的禍，但他以年輕時一件往事說明：歷經歲月後，他最關
心的是——為什麼沒能及時回應他人的需要，為什麼不能及時行善。

演講發表後三個月，他的話全文被紐約時報刊到網站上，一天之內，桑
德斯這則簡單卻振奮人心的小故事，被深受撼動的百萬讀者分享傳播。

為什麼？因為這些話其實是許多人內心對生活的渴望，渴望人與人之
間更多善意，期待與人充實地交流帶來生命的意義。

如今新經典將其編輯成中英文對照版，將這席雋永的講稿獻給即將踏
入社會的年輕人，提醒大家這一生除了勇敢追夢，更要時時讓自己對
世間懷抱著良善之念。這份特別的畢業禮，也許無法讓人成功致富，
但對世人的生命應該有珍貴的價值。恭喜畢業，恭喜。

——新經典文化編輯部

恭喜畢業

離開學校後，最重要的事

桑德斯先生於 2013 年 5 月 11 日為美國雪城大學畢業生致詞演講，
本文是由講稿經修潤編輯而成。

經歷好幾個世代，給大學畢業生做演講慢慢發展出一種模式：邀請某個風光不再，在人生中犯過各種大錯的傻老頭（就像我），讓他們給一群風華正茂、精力旺盛、前途無限的年輕人（就像你們）一點誠心實在的建議。

今天我準備遵照這個模式在此說點話。

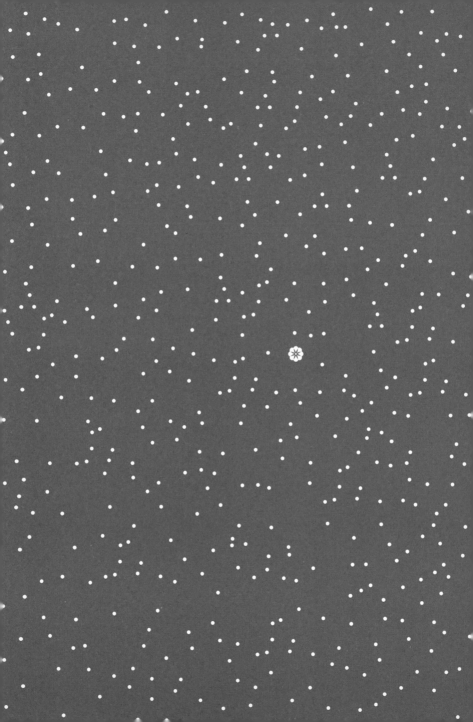

現今，老一輩對年輕人有一大益處，除了向他借錢花，或是請他表演上個時代的舞步，好讓台下的你們邊看邊樂不可支之外，你還可以問問他：「回首過去大半生，你有什麼覺得後悔的？」這個時候，他會有好多話告訴你。

有時候，你知道的，就算你不問，他也會搶著說。甚至你要求他不說，他還是停不住口。

那麼，我後悔些什麼呢？後悔我經常處於貧困？不是。後悔我幹過一些糟透的工作，比方跑去屠宰場裡幫生肉去骨？(而且我完全不想談工作的細節) 也不是。我並不後悔幹過這些事。

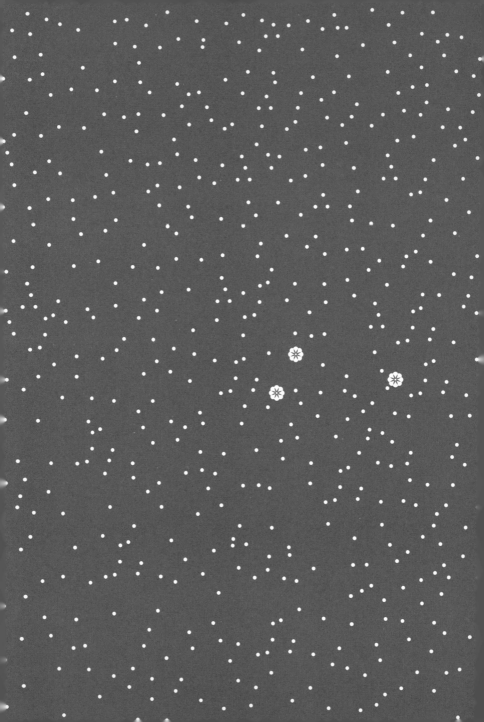

我曾經在蘇門答臘島的河流中裸泳，當時我聽到一陣吵鬧聲，抬頭一看，有三百多隻猴子正坐在河道旁往河裡大便，我嚇得當場張大嘴，一絲不掛地愣在河裡。後來我還因此染上重病，經過整整七個月才痊癒。我會後悔當時下水？現在想想，我不怎麼後悔這檔事。我會後悔做過一些當時讓自己蒙羞的事嗎？比如我在一大群觀眾前打曲棍球，當時我很喜歡的女孩也坐在觀眾席中，一不留神我就摔倒了，就在我哇哇怪叫的同時，還鬼使神差地把那顆球打進了自己隊的球門，球棒被我打飛，奔向觀眾，險些砸中那個女孩。不，我一點也不會把這件事放在心上。

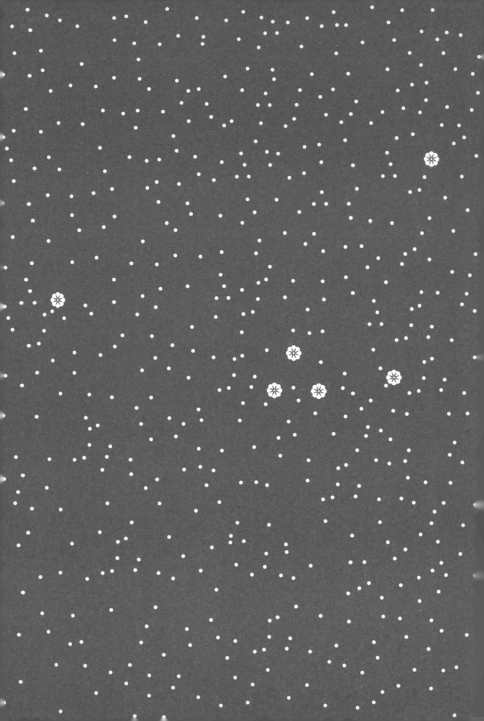

真正讓我後悔莫及的,是這一件事:

那一年我上七年級,班裡轉來了一個新同學。為了保護對方隱私,我在這裡給她暫時取個假名艾倫。艾倫個子很小,而且個性害羞。她戴著藍色像貓眼的眼鏡,那時候只有老太太才會戴這種眼鏡。她很容易緊張,一緊張,她就不由自主地把一絡頭髮咬在嘴裡,不斷嚼來嚼去。

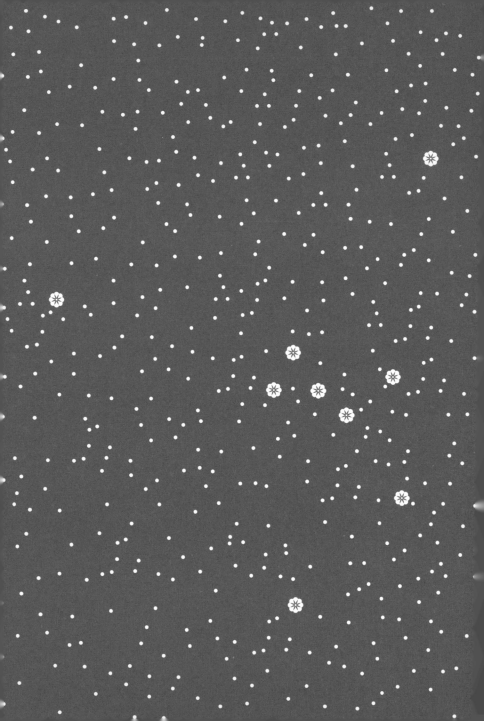

總之，這個艾倫來到我們學校，住進我們的社區，不過人們對她視而不見，還時常嘲笑她(妳的頭髮很好吃吧？——這一類的話)，我知道這些事情傷害著她。我還能記得她被嘲笑侮辱後臉上的神情：低頭望向地面，似乎有點自責，好像被人提醒了她應屬的地位，並且竭盡全力想馬上在人前消失。她會在被嘲弄之後，移步離開，嘴裡依然含著那一綹頭髮。我在自己家裡會想著，如果她放學回家，她媽媽像別人母親一樣問起：「甜心，今天學校開心嗎？」她大概會回答：「嗯，很好。」她媽媽會再問她：「今天交到了朋友嗎？」她則會回答：「對，很多朋友。」

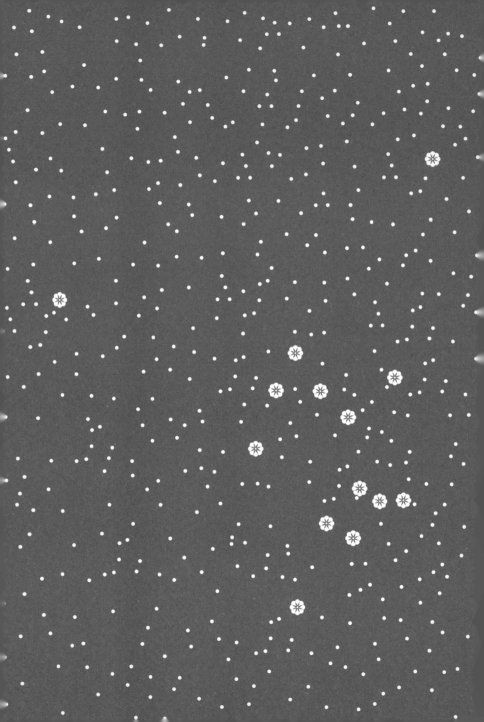

有時候，我看到她獨自一人在自家前院裡踱步不前，似乎害怕離開那個院子。

……後來她們就搬家了。就這樣。沒有發生什麼大悲劇，沒有重大災難。

前一天她還在學校裡，第二天她就不在了。

故事結束了。

現在你們要問，我有什麼好後悔的呢？為什麼四十二年之後，我還對這件事耿耿於懷？相較於學校裡大多數人，我對她算得上友善的。我從未對她出言不遜，甚至有幾次我還稍微挺身為她辯護過。

然而，我就是對這整件事至今耿耿於懷。

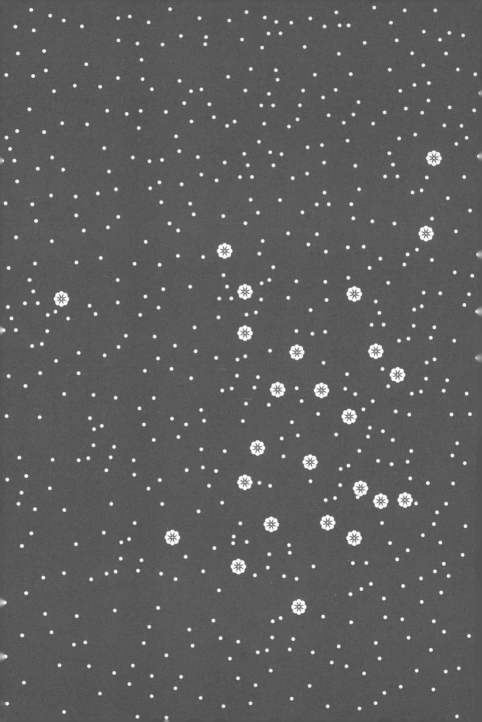

因此，我發現一個真實的道理，雖然聽起來有點老生常談，我也不知道還有什麼高明的說法：

我一生中最後悔的事就是**沒有及時表達對他人的善意**。

當一個遭受痛苦的人在我面前，當這樣的時刻發生時，我的回應卻是……理性克制。沉默緘言。甚至無動於衷。

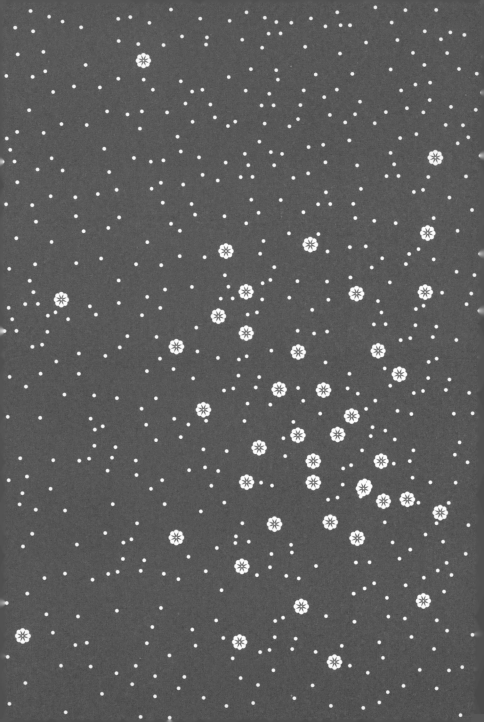

又或者，從事情的另一端來看：誰，在你的生命記憶裡，會讓你深深愛惜惦念著，並對他懷著無庸置疑的溫暖感受？

我相信就是那些對待你最仁慈良善的人。

與人為善看似輕而易舉，實行起來卻困難重重。我覺得，如果把這作為人生的目標，不管怎麼努力，我們常常連「良善一點」都做不好。

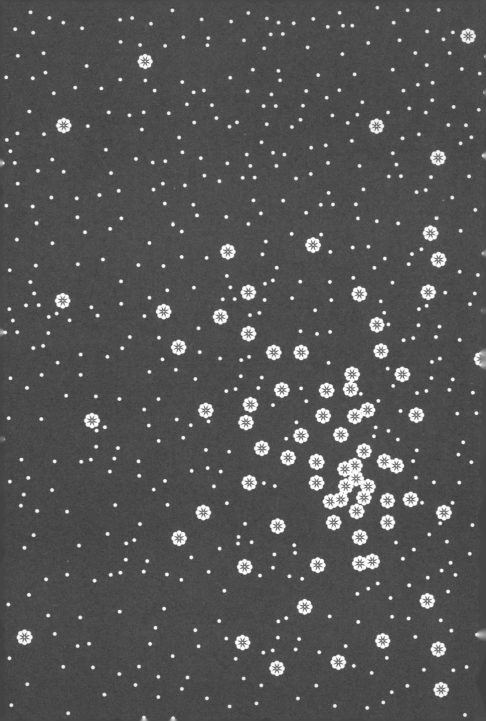

所以，最最重要的問題來了：問題出在哪裡？──為什麼
我們總是不夠良善呢？

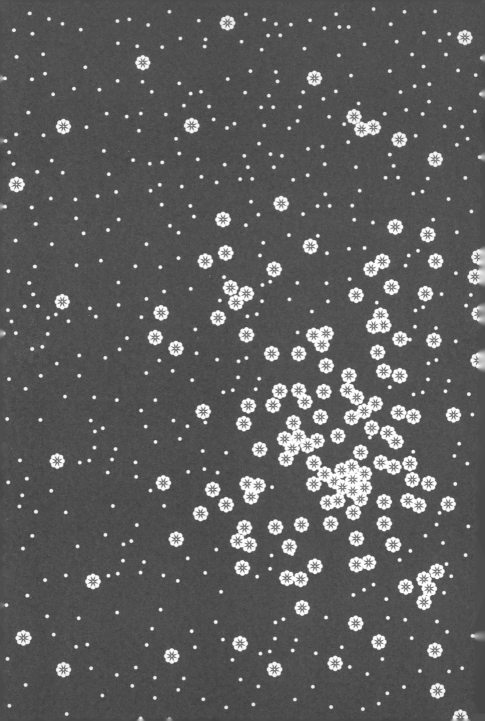

以下是我的看法：

打從出生，我們的腦海中不免帶著一連串與生俱來的錯亂，這大概某種程度上符合達爾文的適者生存法則，帶著錯亂的人才能存活至今。我們搞錯的事情不外乎：

一、我們是宇宙中心 (換句話說，我們覺得自己的故事是唯一的，最重要的，最精彩的)；

二、我們自外於整個宇宙 (先看到我們，然後一切都是其他，其他的萬事萬物都歸入無用之物—狗、鞦韆、內布拉斯加州、低垂的雲，當然，還有其他各國各地方的人民)；

三、我們是永生不死的 (確實有死亡這麼件事，不過，那是發生在別人身上的事情，跟我沒關係)。

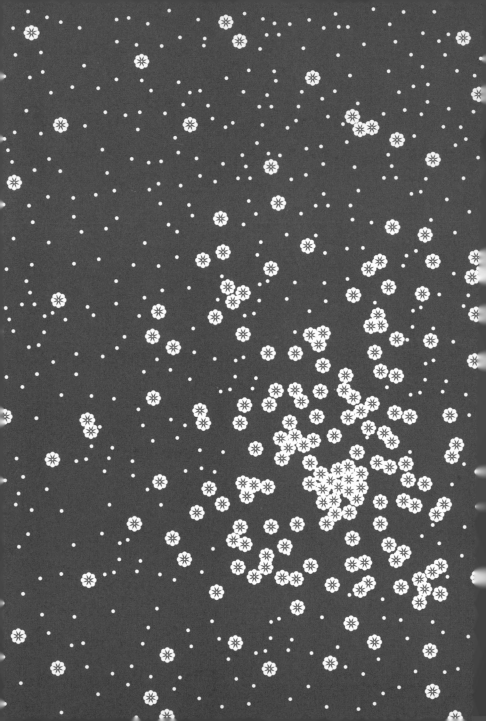

如今，我們不再相信這些——智識上，我們更加成熟了，
然而，這些想法卻深深的烙印在我們心裡，甚至成為我們
的生存準則，這造成我們將自己的需求凌駕於其他人之
上，儘管我們內心真正渴望的是少幾分自私，多關注當下
正在發生的一切，擁有更開闊的心胸、更懂得關愛他人，
等等。

我們想要更良善，因為我們都曾經體驗過那樣的時候，而
且喜歡那種狀況。

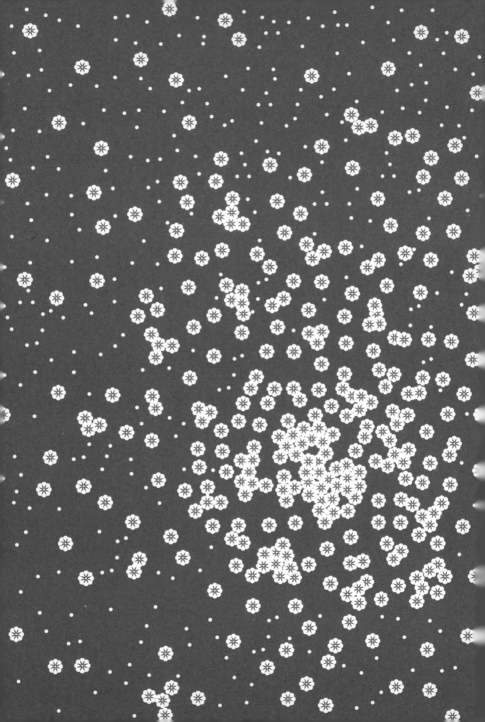

所以第二最最重要的問題是：我們如何才能做到？如何可
能變得更良善，心胸更開闊？怎樣才能少幾分自私？更專
注在當下而不是抱著虛妄的幻想？等等

是的。這是個好問題。

可惜的是，要回答這麼大的問題的我只剩三分鐘了。

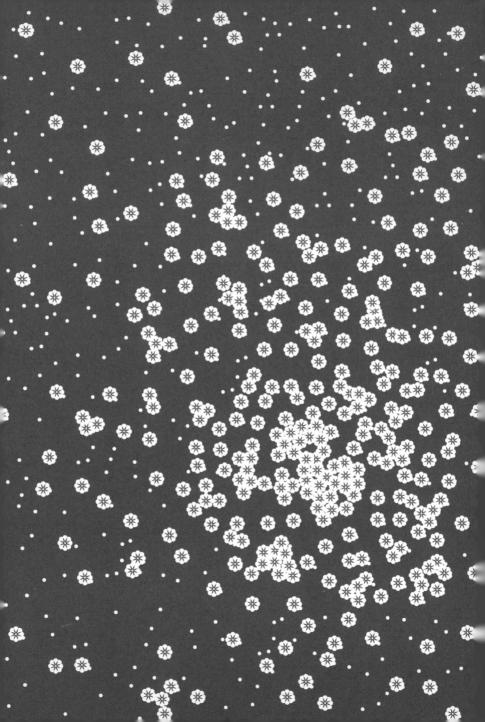

那就讓我這麼說好了：方法是**有的**。而且你們都已經知道了，因為在我們生命中，我們就常常面對**良善活躍階段**和**良善低迷階段**，你們也很清楚自己在何時會趨向前者而遠離後者。我們已觀察到良善是個可變動的項目，這個看法會導致有趣的結果，既然良善是會**增減**的，我們就可以推論它可以被**強化**。也就是說，一定有實踐之道能讓我們時而豐沛時而枯竭的良善之心變得強大而堅定。

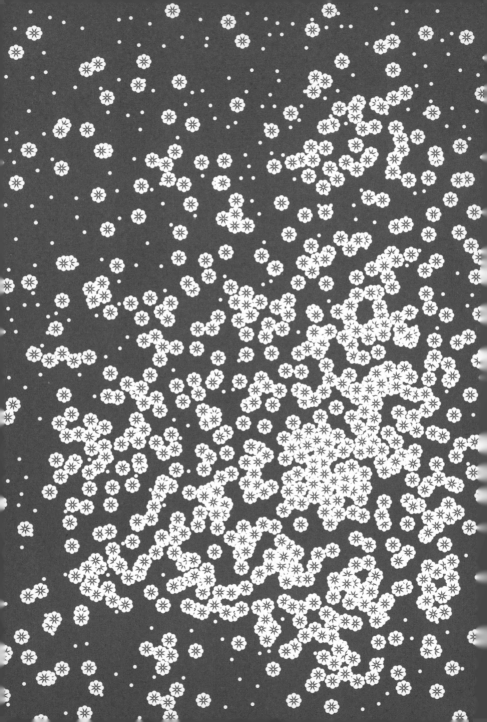

教育就是個好的方法；全心全意投入藝術事業也是好方法；祈禱很好；冥想也可以；與親密的朋友坦誠談話；或者找到一個精神傳統支撐自己──承認一件事，在我們的人生之前就有無數聰明人士也提出過同樣的問題，並為我們留下了寶貴的答案。如果我們不懂得從過往的歷史中找到這些智慧的聲音，那就太可惜也太給自己找死路了。就好像是我們枉顧物理學已有的發現，或者無視於人類醫學上已經研發出的腦部手術，空想著自己重新找出這些學理的奧秘。

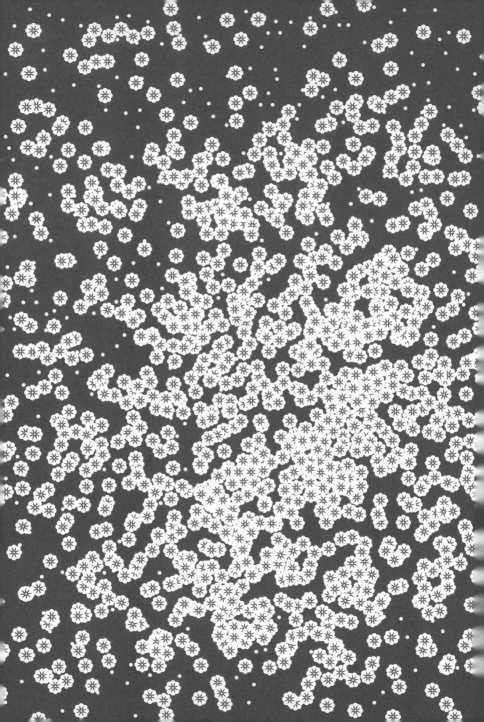

因為，與人為善這件事，其實遠比我們所想的困難——
那起始於我們面對美麗的彩虹、可愛的小狗，慢慢發展到
後來……卻幾乎涵蓋了，沒錯，世間萬物的道理。

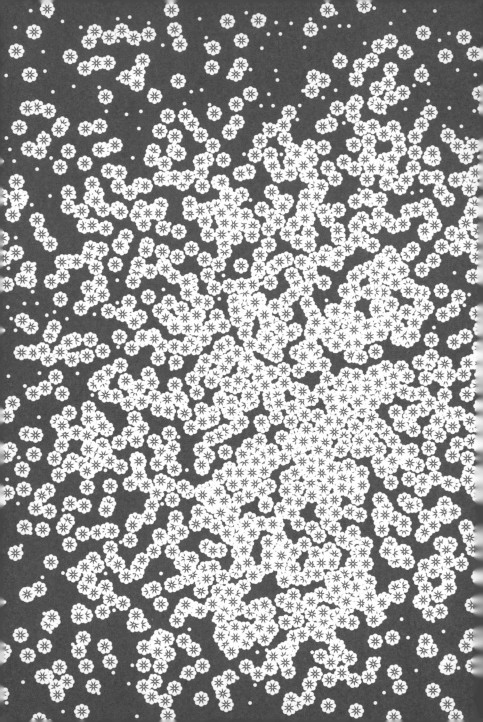

有一個事實對我們是有利的：隨著年齡增加，我們自然就會變得**越來越良善**。也許是單純因為時間消損掉我們內在的自私。當我們逐漸年長，會不斷體悟到自私自利是多麼徒勞無益——感受到這種行為並不合人性邏輯，真的。我們對他人施予愛之時，自我中心主義會受到糾正。人生多有不如意時，當別人為我們辯護，對我們伸出援手時，我們明白我們不是獨立的存在，我們都想融入集體。當我們至親至愛的人一個個離開這個世界，我們慢慢了解到有朝一日我們也會死去 (但仍懷著一種心情：那一天離這一刻的自己還很遙遠)。大多數人都是越年老越善良。我覺得這再明確不過。雪城大學的偉大詩人海頓・卡魯斯在他人生盡頭所完成的一首詩中說：他心裡裝著滿滿的愛，這一刻。

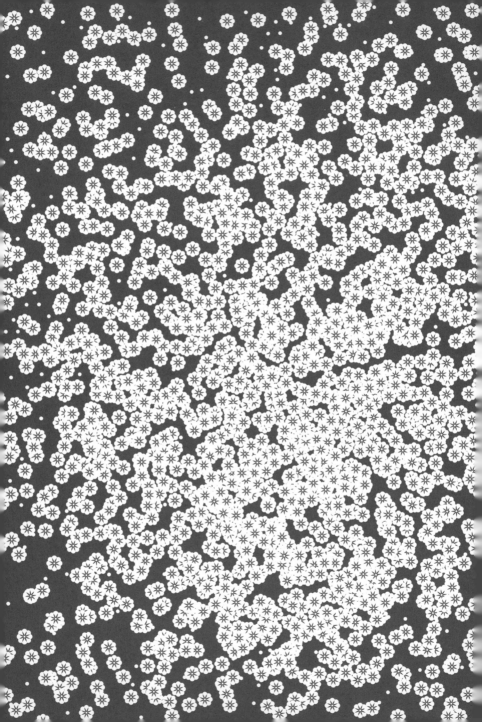

所以，讓我預言，並且滿心地期望，期望你們都會逐漸成熟起來，你們會更無私，更良善，自我中心會漸漸轉化為對他人的愛。如果你有了小孩，屏除自我中心的變化過程會更快更明顯。那時後，為了能讓孩子受益，你會毫不畏懼任何困難。你們的父母現在如此的自豪和快樂，原因就在於此。他們的最大的夢想之一已經實現；因為你們學會了戰勝困難而且已學有所獲。成功讓你們更加成熟。你們未來的生活會充滿陽光，從這一刻開始，直到永遠。

恭喜你們畢業，不過我還要說。

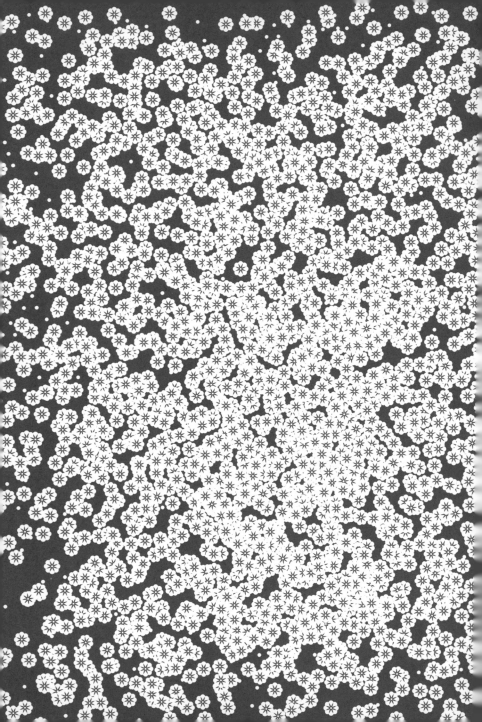

年輕時，我們容易焦慮，因為我們總是懷疑自己把一件事做好的能力。這情緒當然有其道理。我們能否成功？我們能否創造一個有保障的生活？而你們——尤其是出生在這個世代的你們，可能已經發現了這個問題：人的野心周而復始，無窮無盡。你高中學業優秀，一心想進好大學；你大學成績非凡，接著想找個好工作；你在職場業績出色，然後又想著……

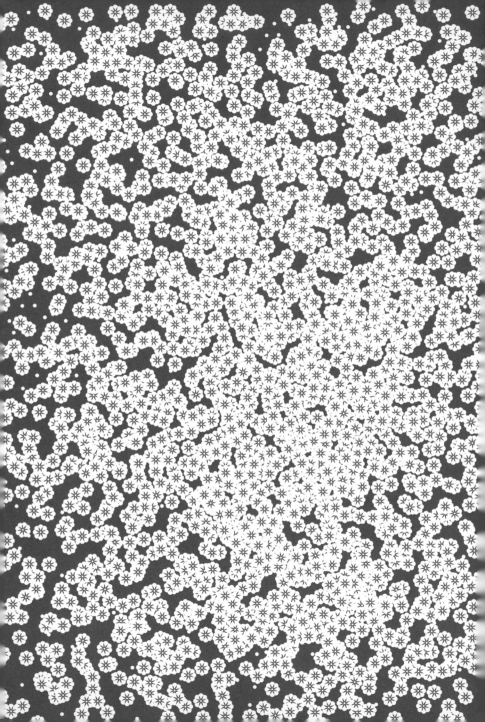

有野心並不是壞事，在我們決心變得良善之際，也同樣包含完成自身的使命。不論你是實業家，功成名就者，還是夢想家。為了成為最出色的自己，我們必須懷抱雄心，把自己最好的一面活出來。

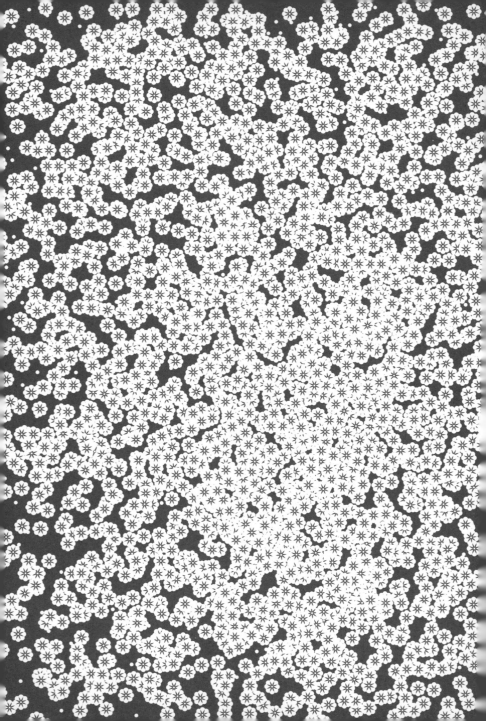

然而，功名是靠不住的。對於「成功」，人人各有定義，成功不但不易，且就算達到了總是還想要更上一層（追求成功猶如攀登一座不斷上升的高山）。而真正危險的是，你的生活完全被成功的追求佔據，而最後你發現，人生巨大的疑問卻始終沒有解答。

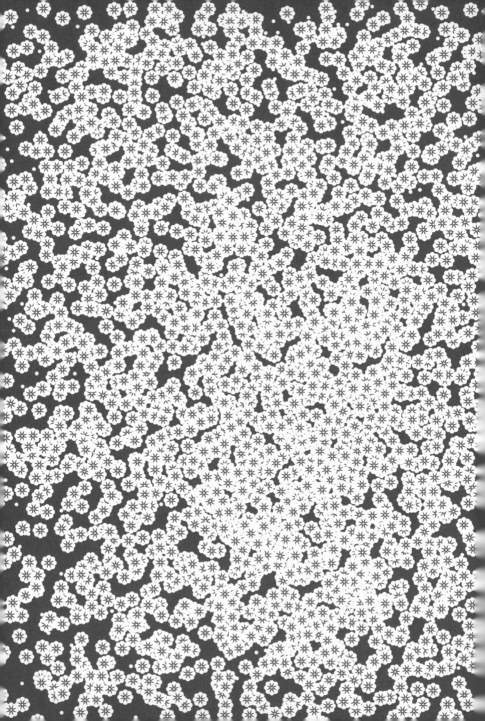

回首我人生的過往，許多事情將我困在雲霧之中，同時讓我把心中的良善一把推得遠遠的。我困在那些焦慮、恐懼、不安，和野心之中，並錯誤地認為只要功成名就就能將這些困擾人的情緒解除。我以為只要我做得更好——更成功、更有錢、更有名——我內心的惶惶不安就會結束。如今我幾乎可以確定，我就是從畢業那一天起，便困在這錯誤的信念中。這麼多年來，我當然心中有著良善之念，但我總是想，先讓我過了這學期、讓我拿到學位、讓我寫完這本書、讓我贏得這個工作任務、讓我買了房、讓我養大孩子 然後，這些事情都做到了，我就會開始對人表現善意，對世界友善。只是，事情沒有結束的時候，只會一件又一件地來，循環無止境，直到……沒完沒了。

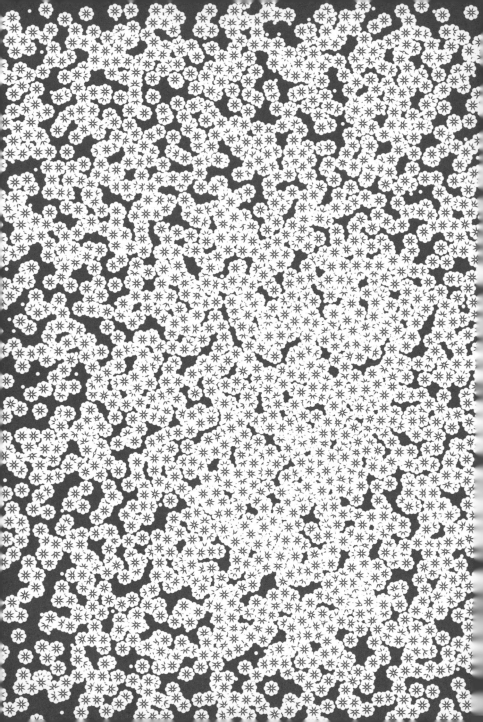

所以，我快點說吧，演講最後我的建議就是：既然人生是一個不斷變良善的過程，不妨調快這個節奏，加快你更良善的步伐，現在就開始做起。雖然我們帶著困惑，身患自私自利這種頑疾，但這並非無解之疾。

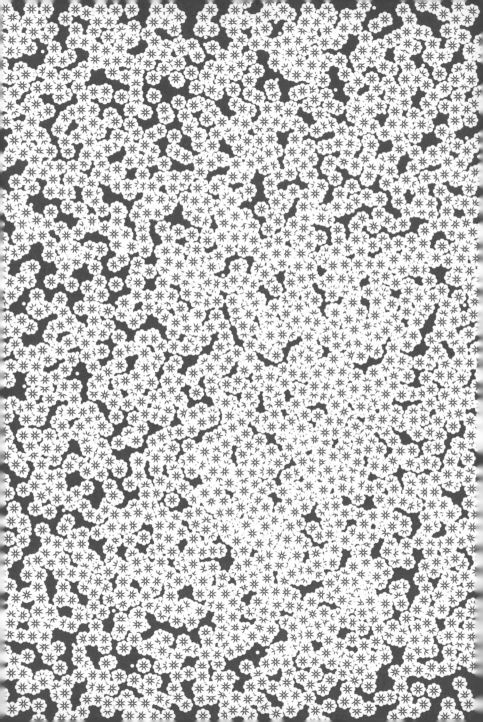

為你自己好，當個好病人，當個積極甚至過分積極都沒關係的病人，努力找尋讓你能不自私的特效藥，在你接下來的人生中，活力滿滿地追求康復。找出怎麼能讓自己更良善的方法，打開自己的心，讓你自身中最能善待他人最慷慨無私的那部分展現出來——全力去做，彷彿人生其他一切都不重要，只有這點至關緊要地全力去做到。

因為，其他一切真的都不重要。

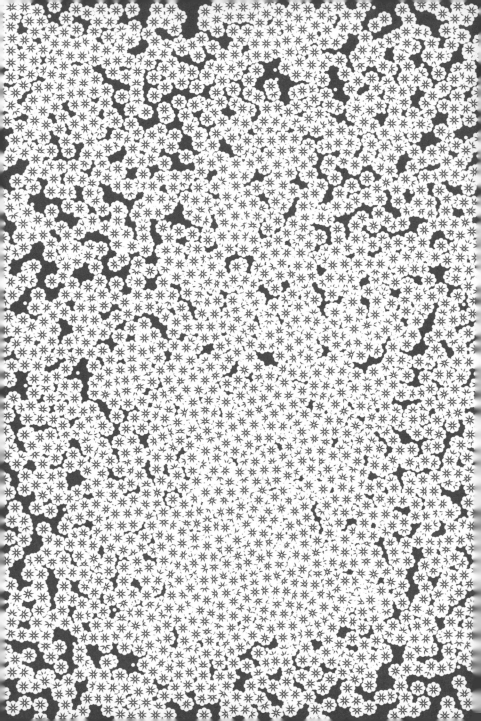

請什麼都去嘗試吧，那些讓你野心勃勃想追逐的夢想——旅遊各地；大把賺錢；成為名人；創新改革；引領時代；陷入情網；創造財富也可以，失去了財富也無妨；或者在叢林河中裸泳（建議提前檢查對猴子糞便的免疫能力）——然而，儘管你竭盡全力讓自己變良善，犯錯也在所難免。我們要把更多精力投入到解決人生中的大問題上，如果只是專注於無聊瑣事，最後只會變得碌碌無為。如果你願意為良善而戰，你閃光的靈魂將掙脫個性缺點的束縛。正如莎士比亞、甘地、德蕾莎修女的靈魂一樣熠熠閃光。越過一切阻撓，到達神聖光明的地方。信仰它的存在，瞭解它，認識它，滋養它，堅持不懈地與人分享它的果實。

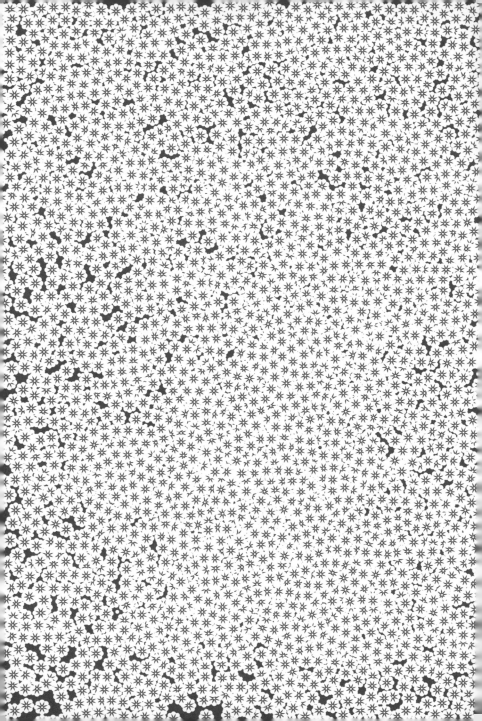

然後到某一天，也許八十年後，當你們一百歲，我
一百三十四歲時，當我們良善得都讓人覺得受不了時，請
給我寫封信，講講你們的生活。我希望聽到你們說：人生
真美好。

我祝福大家幸福滿溢，願大家幸運常伴，並度過一個美好的夏天。

Congratulations, by the way

Down through the ages, a traditional form has evolved for this type of speech, which is: Some old fart, his best years behind him, who over the course of his life, has made a series of dreadful mistakes (that would be me), gives heartfelt advice to a group of shining, energetic young people, with all of their best years ahead of them (that would be you).

And I intend to respect that tradition.

Now, one useful thing you can do with an old person, in addition to borrowing money from them, or asking them to do one of their old-time "dances," so you can watch, while laughing, is ask: "Looking back, what do you regret?" And they'll tell you. Sometimes, as you know, they'll tell you even if you haven't asked. Sometimes, even when you've specifically requested they not tell you, they'll tell you. So: What do I regret? Being poor from time to time? Not really. Working terrible jobs, like "knuckle-puller in a slaughterhouse" ? (And don't even ASK what that entails.) No. I don't regret that.

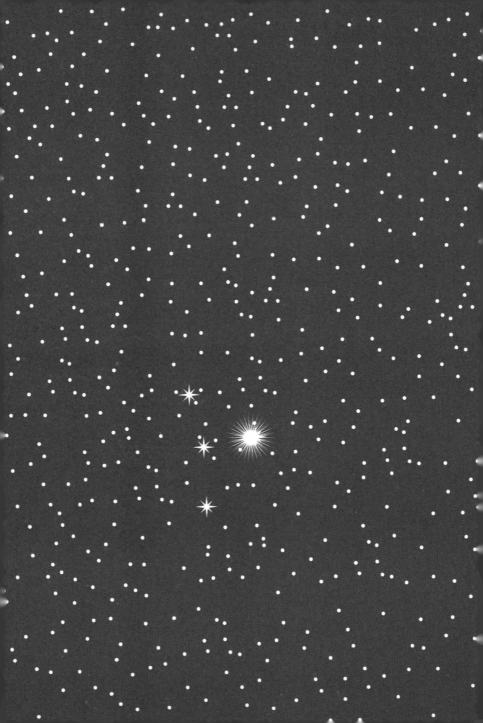

Skinny-dipping in a river in Sumatra, a little buzzed, and looking up and seeing like 300 monkeys sitting on a pipeline, pooping down into the river, the river in which I was swimming, with my mouth open, naked? And getting deathly ill afterwards, and staying sick for the next seven months? Not so much. Do I regret the occasional humiliation? Like once, playing hockey in front of a big crowd, including this girl I really liked, I somehow managed, while falling and emitting this weird whooping noise, to score on my own goalie, while also sending my stick flying into the crowd, nearly hitting that girl? No. I don't even regret that.

But here's something I do regret:

In seventh grade, this new kid joined our class. In the interest of confidentiality, her Convocation Speech name will be "ELLEN." ELLEN was small, shy. She wore these blue cat's-eye glasses that, at the time, only old ladies wore. When nervous, which was pretty much always, she had a habit of taking a strand of hair into her mouth and chewing on it.

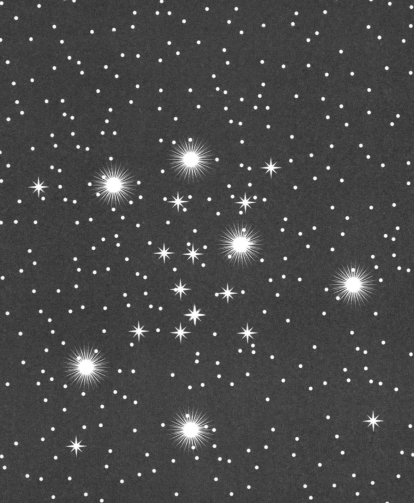

So she came to our school and our neighborhood, and was mostly ignored, occasionally teased ("Your hair taste good?" —that sort of thing). I could see this hurt her. I still remember the way she'd look after such an insult: eyes cast down, a little gut-kicked, as if, having just been reminded of her place in things, she was trying, as much as possible, to disappear. After awhile she'd drift away, hair-strand still in her mouth. At home, I imagined, after school, her mother would say, you know: "How was your day, sweetie?" and she'd say, "Oh, fine." And her mother would say, "Making any friends?" and she'd go, "Sure, lots."

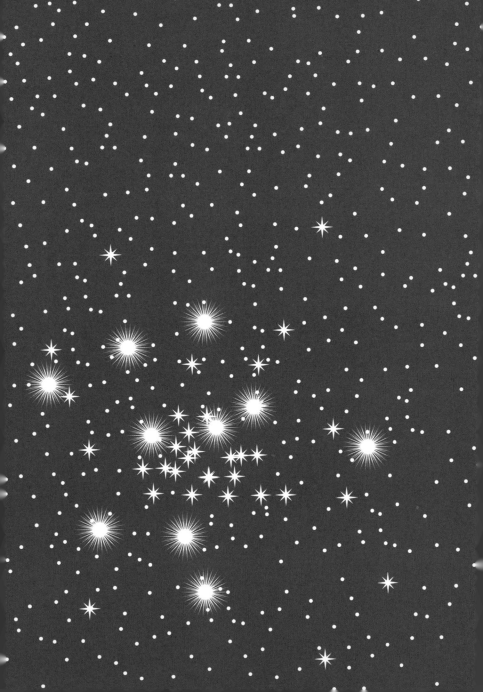

Sometimes I'd see her hanging around alone
in her front yard, as if afraid to leave it.

And then—they moved. That was it.
No tragedy, no big final hazing.

One day she was there, next day she wasn't.

End of story.

Now, why do I regret *that*? Why, forty-two years
later, am I still thinking about it? Relative to most
of the other kids, I was actually pretty *nice* to
her. I never said an unkind word to her. In fact,
I sometimes even (mildly) defended her.

But still. It bothers me.

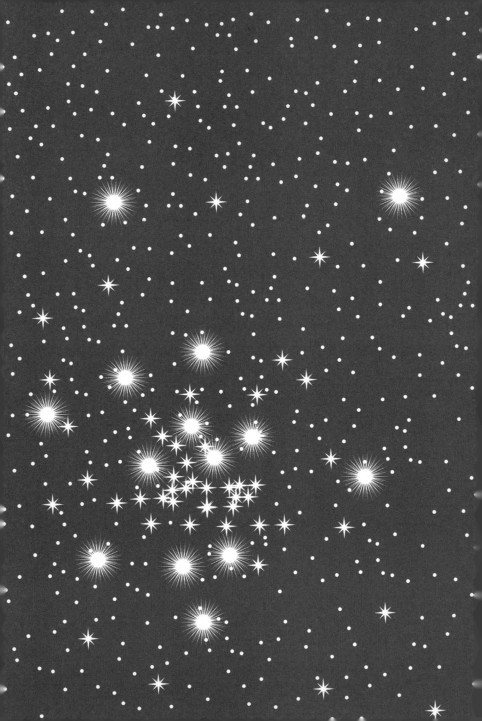

So here's something I know to be true, although it's a little corny, and I don't quite know what to do with it:

What I regret most in my life are *failures of kindness*.

Those moments when another human being was there, in front of me, suffering, and I responded . . . sensibly. Reservedly. Mildly.

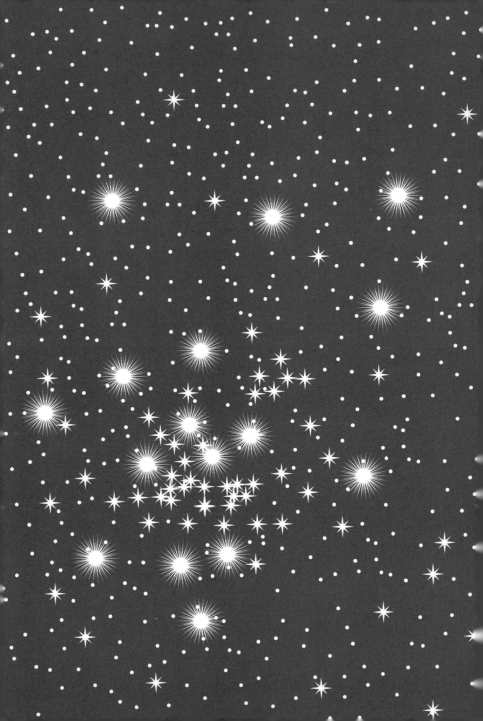

Or, to look at it from the other end of the telescope:
Who, in your life, do you remember most fondly,
with the most undeniable feelings of warmth?

Those who were kindest to you, I bet.

It's a little facile, maybe, and certainly hard
to implement, but I'd say, as a goal in life,
you could do worse than: *Try to be kinder*.

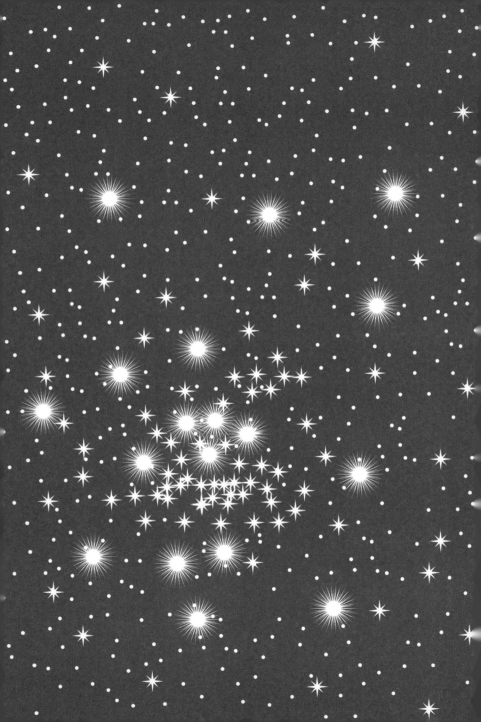

Now, the million-dollar question: What's our problem—Why aren't we kinder?

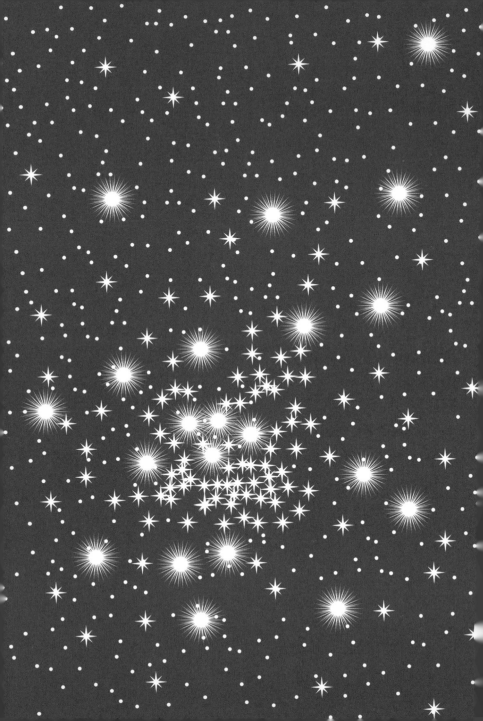

Here's what I think:

Each of us is born with a series of built-in confusions
that are probably somehow Darwinian. These are: (1)
we're central to the universe (that is, our personal story
is the main and most interesting story, the *only* story,
really); (2) we're separate from the universe (there's *us*
and then, out there, all that other junk—dogs and swing
sets, and the State of Nebraska and low-hanging clouds
and, you know, other people), and (3) we're permanent
(death is real, O.K., sure—for you, but not for me).

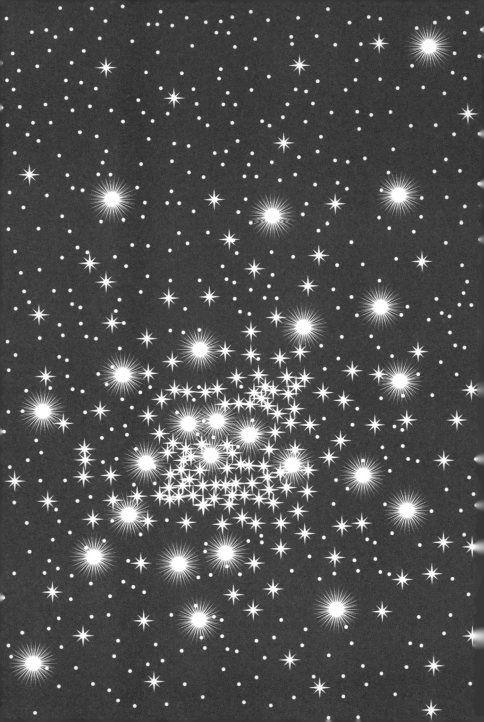

Now, we don't really believe these things—intellectually we know better—but we believe them viscerally, and live by them, and they cause us to prioritize our own needs over the needs of others, even though what we really want, in our hearts, is to be less selfish, more aware of what's actually happening in the present moment, more open, and more loving.

We know we want to be these things because from time to time we *have been* these things—and liked it.

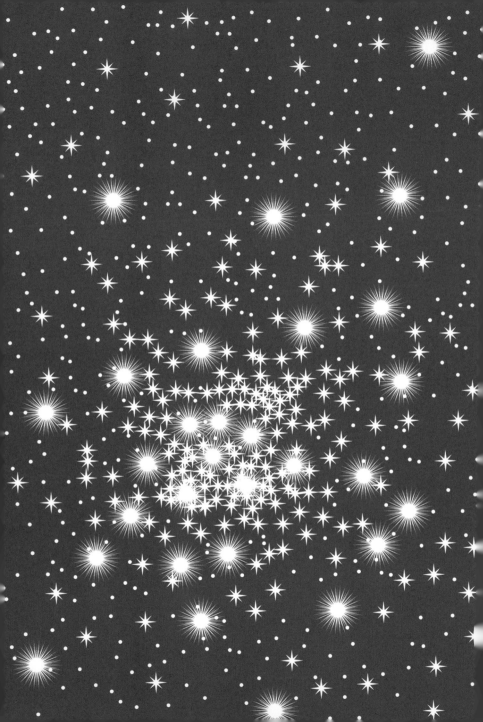

So, the second million-dollar question: How might we DO this? How might we become more loving, more open, less selfish, more present, less delusional, etc., etc?

Well, yes, good question.

Unfortunately, I only have three minutes left.

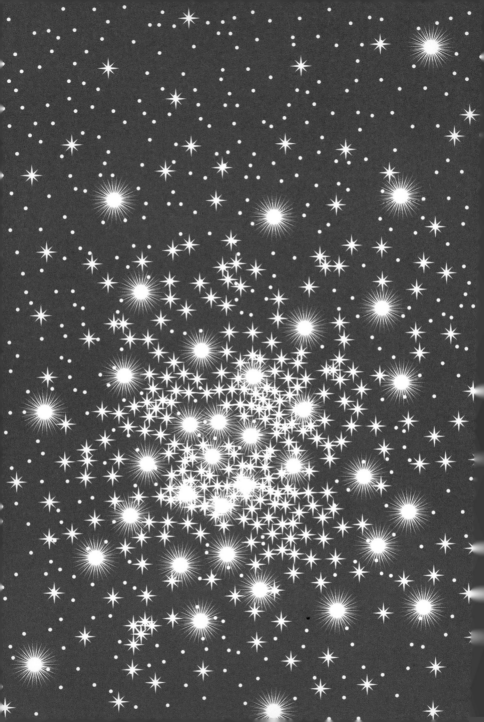

So let me just say this. There *are* ways. You already
know that because, in your life, there have been
High Kindness periods and Low Kindness periods,
and you know what inclined you toward the former
and away from the latter. It's an exciting idea: Since
we have observedthat kindness is *variable*, we might
also sensibly conclude that it is *improvable*; that is,
there must be approaches and practices that can
actually increase our ambient level of kindness.

97

Education is good; immersing ourselves in a work of art: good; prayer is good; meditation's good; a frank talk with a dear friend; establishing ourselves in some kind of spiritual tradition—recognizing that there have been countless really smart people before us who have asked these same questions and left behind answers for us. It would be strange and self-defeating to fail to seek out these wise voices from the past—as self-defeating as it would be to attempt to rediscover the principles of physics from scratch or invent a new method of brain surgery without having learned the ones that already exist.

99

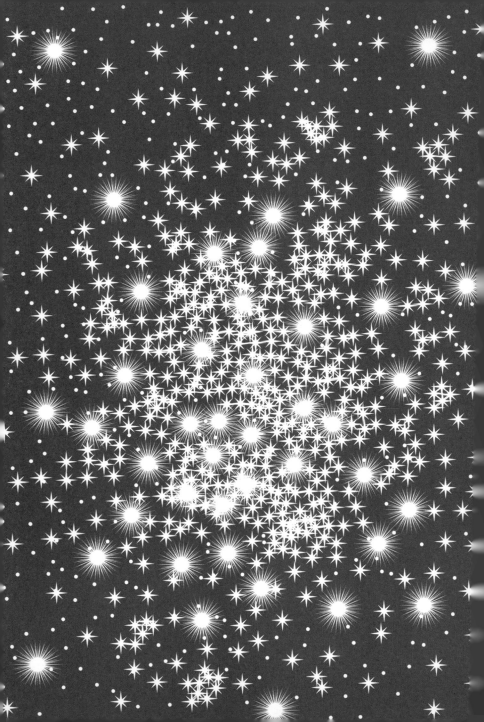

Because kindness, it turns out, is hard—
it starts out all rainbows and puppy dogs, and
expands to include . . . well, everything.

One thing in our favor: some of this "becoming kinder" happens naturally, with age. It might be a simple matter of attrition: as we get older, we come to see how useless it is to be selfish—how illogical, really. We come to love other people and are thereby counter-instructed in our own centrality. We get our butts kicked by real life, and people come to our defense, and help us, and we learn that we're not separate, and don't want to be. We see people near and dear to us dropping away, and are gradually convinced that maybe we too will drop away (someday, a long time from now). Most people, as they age, become less selfish and more loving. I think this is true. The great Syracuse poet Hayden Carruth said, in a poem written near the end of his life, that he was "mostly Love, now."

And so, a prediction, and my heartfelt wish for you: as you get older, your self will diminish and you will grow in love. YOU will gradually be replaced by LOVE. If you have kids, that will be a huge moment in your process of self-diminishment. You really won't care what happens to YOU, as long as they benefit. That's one reason your parents are so proud and happy today. One of their fondest dreams has come true: you have accomplished something difficult and tangible that has enlarged you as a person and will make your life better, from here on in, forever.

Congratulations, by the way.

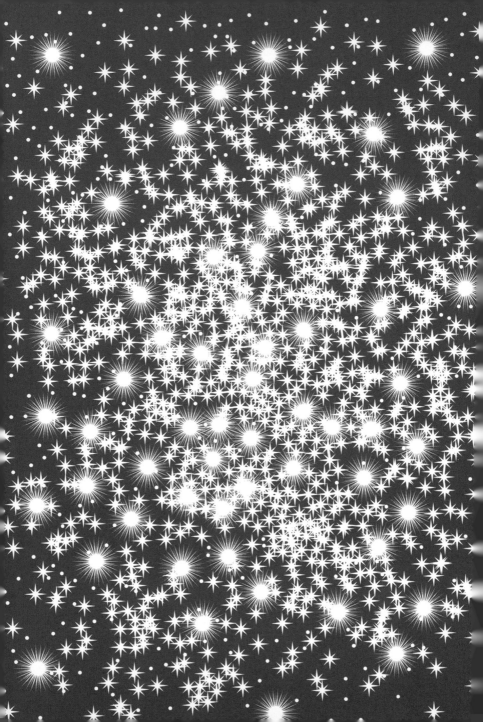

When young, we're anxious—understandably—to find out if we've got what it takes. Can we succeed? Can we build a viable life for ourselves? But you—in particular you, of this generation—may have noticed a certain cyclical quality to ambition. You do well in high-school, in hopes of getting into a good college, so you can do well in the good college, in the hopes of getting a good job, so you can do well in the good job so you can . . .

And this is actually O.K. If we're going to become kinder, that process has to include taking ourselves seriously—as doers, as accomplishers, as dreamers. We have to do that, to be our best selves.

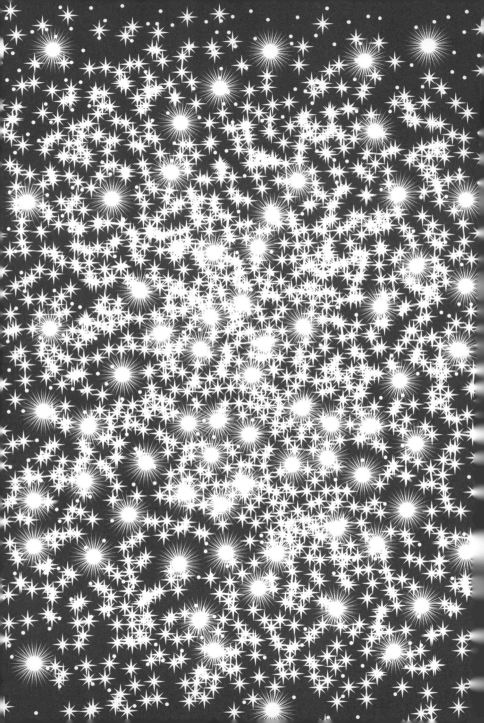

Still, accomplishment is unreliable. "Succeeding," whatever that might mean to you, is hard, and the need to do so constantly renews itself (success is like a mountain that keeps growing ahead of you as you hike it), and there's the very real danger that "succeeding" will take up your whole life, while the big questions go untended.

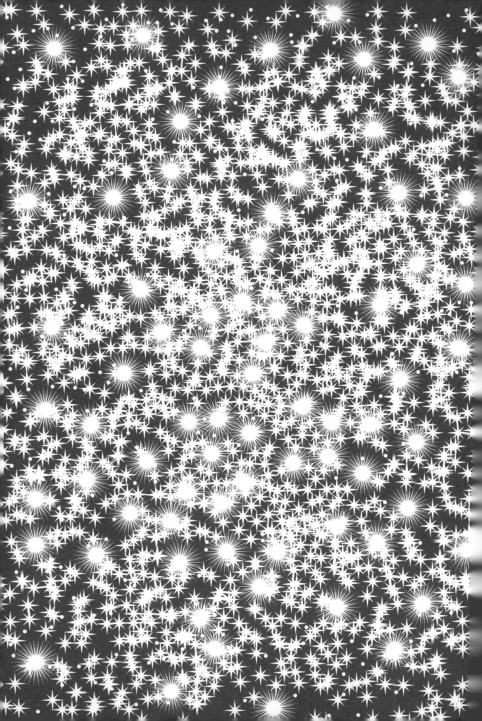

I can look back and see that I've spent much of my life in a cloud of things that have tended to push "being kind" to the periphery. Things like: Anxiety. Fear. Insecurity. Ambition. The mistaken belief that enough accomplishment will rid me of all that anxiety, fear, insecurity, and ambition. The belief that if I can only *accrue* enough—enough accomplishment, money, fame—my neuroses will disappear. I've been in this fog certainly since, at least, my own graduation day. Over the years I've felt: Kindness, sure—but first let me finish this semester, this degree, this book; let me succeed at this job, and afford this house, and raise these kids, and then, finally, when all is acomplished, I'll get started on the kindness. Except it never all gets accomplished. It's a cycle that can go on . . . well, forever.

So, quick, end-of-speech advice: Since, according
to me, your life is going to be a gradual process of
becoming kinder and more loving: Hurry up. Speed it
along. Start right now. There's a confusion in each of us,
a sickness, really: selfishness. But there's also a cure.

Be a good and proactive and even somewhat desperate patient on your own behalf—seek out the most efficacious anti-selfishness medicines, energetically, for the rest of your life. Find out what makes you kinder, what opens you up and brings out the most loving, generous, and unafraid version of you—and go after those things as if nothing else matters.

Because, actually, nothing else does.

Do all the other things, the ambitious things—travel, get rich, get famous, innovate, lead, fall in love, make and lose fortunes, swim naked in wild jungle rivers (after first having it tested for monkey poop)—but as you do, to the extent that you can, err in the direction of kindness. Do those things that incline you toward the big questions, and avoid the things that would reduce you and make you trivial. That luminous part of you that exists beyond personality—your soul, if you will—is as bright and shining as any that has ever been. Bright as Shakespeare's, bright as Gandhi's, bright as Mother Teresa's. Clear away everything that keeps you separate from this secret luminous place. Believe it exists, come to know it better, nurture it, share its fruits tirelessly.

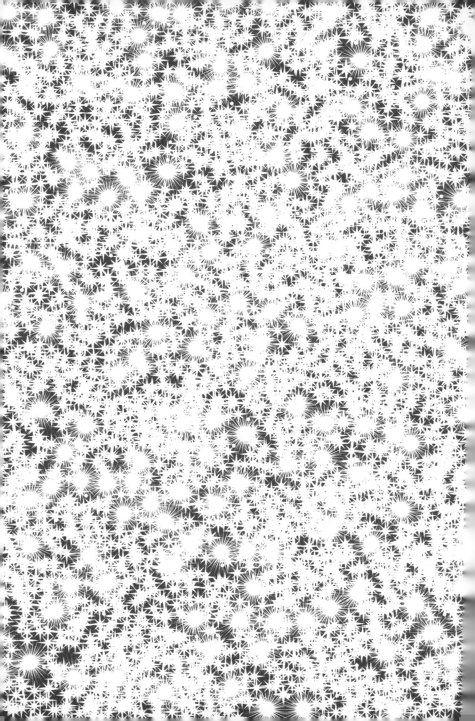

And someday, in 80 years, when you're 100, and I'm 134, and we're both so kind and loving we're nearly unbearable, drop me a line, let me know how your life has been. I hope you will say: It has been so wonderful.

I wish you great happiness, all the luck in the world, and a beautiful summer.

Essential YY0906

恭喜畢業
離開學校後，最重要的事
Congratulations, by the way

作者

喬治‧桑德斯（George Saunders, 1958-）

桑德斯出版了超過十二本短篇小說，從一九九二年起他就持續為《紐約客》寫了多篇 Shouts & Murmurs。代表作有短篇集入圍海明威小說獎的 CivilWarLand in Bad Decline，以 Pastoralia 入圍國家書卷獎且拿下 Folio大獎。二○一四年以這本非小說《恭喜畢業：離開學校後，最重要的事》登上紐約時報暢銷榜，這本書是收錄他在二○一三年美東雪城 (Syracuse) 大學畢業典禮上所做的講演稿。

譯者

徐之野

台大外文系畢業，喜歡英美文學作品，譯有《大亨小傳》。

ThinKingDom 新經典文化

發行人　葉美瑤

封面內頁設計　陳文德
行銷企劃　傅恩群
編務協力　詹修蘋、王琦柔
版權負責　陳柏昌
副總編輯　梁心愉

出版　新經典圖文傳播有限公司
地址　臺北市中正區重慶南路一段五七號十一樓之四
電話　02-2331-1830　傳真　02-2331-1831
讀者服務信箱　thinkingdomtw@gmail.com
FB粉絲團　https://www.facebook.com/thinkingdomtw?ref=ts

總經銷　高寶書版集團
地址　臺北市內湖區洲子街八八號三樓
電話　02-2799-2788　傳真　02-2799-0909

海外總經銷　時報文化出版企業股份有限公司
地址　桃園縣龜山鄉萬壽路一段三五一號
電話　02-2306-6842　傳真　02-2304-9301

初版二刷　二○一五年四月十五日
定價　新臺幣二八○元

版權所有，不得轉載、複製、翻印，違者必究
裝訂錯誤或破損的書，請寄回新經典文化更換

恭喜畢業──離開學校後，最重要的事
/ 喬治‧桑德斯(George Saunders)著；徐之野譯.
— 初版. — 臺北市：新經典圖文傳播，2015.04
128面；13.5x19公分.—（Essential；YY0906）
譯自：Congratulations, by the way : some thoughts on kindness
ISBN 978-986-5824-38-9(精裝)

1.修身
192.1　　　　　　　　　　　　104003652